# The Three Bears

## Fairy Tale Classics

retold by Dandi

here once lived a quite content family of bear,

And a most spunky gal who had curls in her hair.

Papa Bear was gigantic, and Mama was tall.

But the wee, little Bear barely made noise at all.

In their little old cottage, those three charming bears

Had three couches, three soup bowls, three beds, and three chairs.

Papa Bear's things were giant, and Baby's were small.

Mama Bear liked the middle-sized stuff most of all.

 hen one day Mama Bear made the porridge too hot.

"Let's go walking," she said, "while I cool this hot pot."

So the three furry bears lumbered out for a stroll.

Now we turn to a Golden-Haired girl and her role.

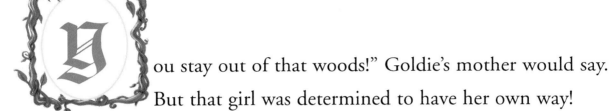 ou stay out of that woods!" Goldie's mother would say.

But that girl was determined to have her own way!

So she chanced on Bear Cottage, and our heroine

Tried the windows, the keyhole — and then she walked in!

"Oh I know that I shouldn't, but now that I'm here,

No one's home, and I guess I have nothing to fear."

o she tasted the porridge of big Papa Bear.

"It's too hot!" she cried out. "I had better beware."

Then she tried to eat Mama's, but found it too cold,

Till at last she found Baby's. (That girl was so bold!)

Well, the girl took a bite, and she sat down to sup.

"My, my, this one's just right! I shall eat it all up."

ut this chair is too big, and the other too tall."

So she sat in the small chair and had a small fall!

"All this work makes me tired," that Golden girl said.

Then she walked up the stairs and went straight to a bed.

Well, she didn't like Papa or Mama Bear's bed.

So she lay in the wee, little Bear's bed instead.

hen the bears found the mess in the kitchen, they knew.

"Someone ate from my porridge!"

"Someone ate from mine too!"

And when wee, little bear saw his porridge all gone,

How he fussed and he fumed! Oh, that bear carried on!

ome sit, Son. It's all right," said that huge Papa Bear.

Then he thundered, "I think someone sat in my chair!"

Mama Bear thought so too, so they looked all around.

But when Baby Bear sat, he plopped flat on the ground!

In his wee, little voice (though the volume increases),

He screamed, "Look at my chair! Someone broke it to pieces!"

**W**ell, they ran to the bedroom, each bear to his bed.

And when Papa saw his, he just shook that bear head.

"I know someone's been sleeping in my bed!" he swore.

"And in mine," said his wife in a middle-sized roar.

aby Bear found the girl sound asleep in his bed.

"I think I've solved the mystery," Baby Bear said.

"I know who," said wee Bear. "And I even know how.
She was sleeping in my bed. And here she is now!"

**W**ell, when Golden-Hair heard that, she opened her eyes.

And that golden-haired girl sure was in for surprise.

At the sight of the bears, Goldie turned tail and ran.

And the family of bears never saw her again.